Melody Of Fear

Mrigendra Bharti

Published by Sellbrochure Vymish Entertainment, 2024.

This is a work of fiction. Similarities to real people, places, or events are entirely coincidental.

MELODY OF FEAR

First edition. July 3, 2024.

Copyright © 2024 Mrigendra Bharti.

ISBN: 979-8227244611

Written by Mrigendra Bharti.

Table of Contents

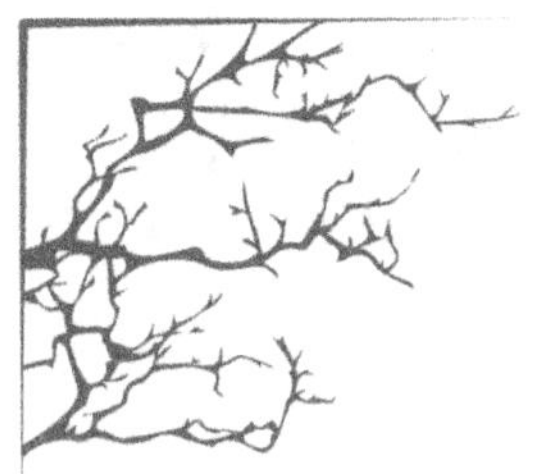

Preface

In the heart of an ancient forest, nestled amidst towering oaks and whispering pines, lies a village steeped in folklore and moonlight melodies. Here, the villagers live in harmony with nature, their peaceful existence protected by generations of brave heroes and the enchanting music that pulses through their very veins. But whispers of a forgotten darkness begin to stir, carried on the chilling wind that creeps from the depths of the woods.

This tale follows the journey of Arjun, a young villager whose heart beats in rhythm with the melodies, and Anya, a skilled warrior with a thirst for knowledge of the past. Together, they face a haunting melody – a melody of fear. It beckons from the crumbling ruins of a long-lost palace, a place where shadows hold dominion and a chilling truth lies buried.

As they delve deeper into the heart of darkness, Arjun and Anya must confront terrifying creatures born from the shadows and uncover the secrets of the forgotten past. Their journey will test their courage, challenge their beliefs, and force them to confront the very essence of fear. Can their melodies of moonlight pierce the veil of darkness? Or will the shadows consume them all, turning the once harmonious melody of their village into a chilling echo of despair?

Prepare to be swept away on a thrilling adventure where courage clashes with terror, and moonlight melodies become the only weapon against the encroaching darkness.

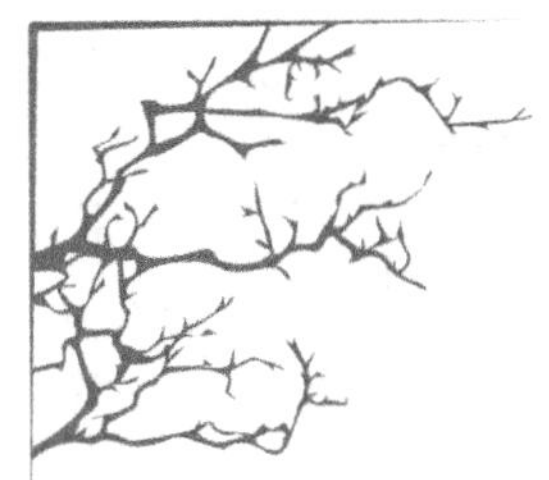

Prologue

The wind howled a mournful song through the skeletal branches of the ancient forest. Beneath a sky choked with swirling clouds, a lone figure trudged towards the crumbling ruins that marked the edge of a forgotten kingdom. Her cloak, once a vibrant crimson, hung in tattered shreds, mirroring the decay that had consumed the land.

This was Elara, the last Queen of Light. Her golden hair, once a crown of defiance, now resembled tangled straw. The moonlight, her only companion, cast an ethereal glow upon her ravaged face, etching deep lines of sorrow and despair.

Years ago, this very land had thrummed with vitality. Now, it was a wasteland, shrouded in an unnatural darkness that devoured all hope. The source of this darkness, a twisted entity of her own creation, festered deep within the ruins. Its chilling laughter echoed through the desolate landscape, a constant reminder of her failure.

Elara clutched a shimmering staff, its once brilliant crystal now dulled and cracked. It was a symbol of her power, now a useless relic. Tears, icy and sharp, traced paths down her dirt-streaked cheeks.

Tonight, driven by a desperate hope, she returned. Not to reclaim her kingdom, for that was lost. But to set in motion a final act of defiance, a melody of sacrifice that might, just might, offer a flicker of redemption in the eternal darkness.

As she entered the ruins, the air grew thick and oppressive. Jagged shadows danced on the crumbling walls, mocking her every step. The laughter of the darkness grew louder, a grotesque symphony of malice.

Elara knew she wouldn't survive the night. But perhaps, just perhaps, her sacrifice would ignite a spark, a melody of hope that would echo through the ages. A hope that someday, the darkness might be banished, and the land would reclaim its lost light. With a final, trembling breath, Elara raised her staff, channeling the last vestiges of her power. The melody she unleashed wasn't a song of war, but a lament, a mournful plea for a future brighter than the shadows that had consumed her. It resonated through the ruins, a defiant whisper against the all-encompassing darkness.

The darkness writhed, its laughter turning into a shriek of frustration. Then, a deafening silence descended. Whether Elara's sacrifice had bought precious time or was a mere footnote in the darkness' reign, only time would tell. But one thing was certain: a melody of hope had been woven into the very fabric of the land, waiting for the day it would rise again.

About Sellbrochure Vymish Entertainment

Sellbrochure Vymish Entertainment, recognized as India's largest book publishing company, has made significant strides in ensuring its extensive collection of books reaches audiences across the global market. This rapid expansion is a testament to the company's dedication to disseminating knowledge and literature far beyond national borders. Central to its success is its affiliation with InkWhirl Media Networks, a reputable entity in the media and publication industry known for its innovative and strategic approaches. Within this network, InkWhirl Publication LLC operates as a vital division, further enhancing the company's capabilities and reach in the international market.

The visionary behind this enterprise is Mrigendra Bharti, the founder of Sellbrochure Vymish Entertainment. His foresight and passion for the literary world have been instrumental in steering the company towards remarkable growth and recognition. Under his leadership, Sellbrochure Vymish Entertainment has not only expanded its catalog but also established a strong presence in both domestic and international markets. Mrigendra Bharti's commitment to excellence and innovation has been a driving force in the company's journey, ensuring that it stays ahead of industry trends and meets the evolving needs of readers worldwide.

Sellbrochure Vymish Entertainment operates under the robust support of its parental organization, Mrigendra Bharti Group InfoTech. This affiliation provides the necessary resources and strategic guidance, enabling the publishing company to undertake ambitious projects and explore new markets. Mrigendra Bharti Group InfoTech's extensive experience in technology and information services has been a valuable asset, allowing Sellbrochure Vymish Entertainment to integrate advanced digital solutions in its operations, thereby enhancing its distribution capabilities and reader engagement.

Through relentless efforts and a commitment to quality, Sellbrochure Vymish Entertainment continues to break barriers and expand the reach of Indian literature globally. The company's diverse portfolio includes a wide range of genres, catering to different age groups and interests, thereby fostering a rich and inclusive reading culture. As it continues to innovate and grow, Sellbrochure Vymish Entertainment remains dedicated to its mission of making literature accessible to all, contributing significantly to the global literary landscape.

Connect With Mrigendra,
Thank you very much for choosing this book.
You can also connect with me on Instagram,
https://www.instagram.com/i_mrigendrabharti.official
With Love,
Mrigendra Bharti

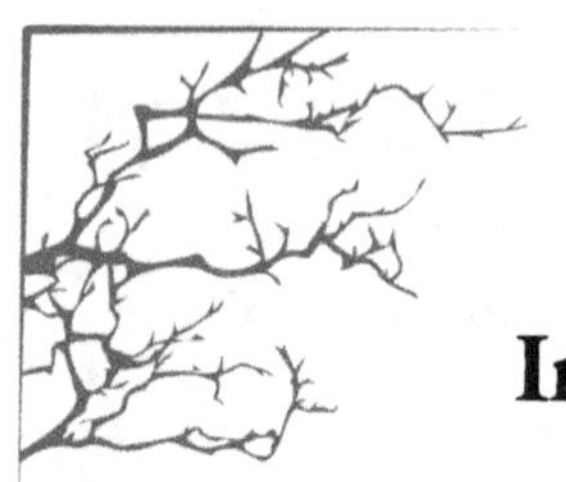

Introduction

Nestled within the emerald embrace of an ancient forest, the village of Eldoria thrived. Here, nestled amongst towering oaks and whispering pines, generations lived in harmony with nature.

The air hummed with an unseen melody, a vibration felt as much as heard, that resonated within the very core of every villager. These were the moonlight melodies, a legacy whispered through the ages, granting them a connection to the land and a defense against the unseen.

Arjun, a young villager with eyes the color of sun-dappled leaves, walked hand-in-hand with Anya, a warrior with the grace of a wildcat and a mind as sharp as her blade. Their laughter echoed through the trees as they practiced swordplay, the rhythmic clang of metal a counterpoint to the unseen melody that pulsed around them.

But whispers of a forgotten darkness began to stir, carried on the chilling wind that crept from the depths of the woods. Unease settled upon the village like a shroud. The elders spoke of a time before, a time when shadows threatened to engulf their light. And tonight, beneath the watchful gaze of a waning moon, an unsettling tremor shook the very ground beneath their feet. It was a chilling reminder of the fragility of their peace, a harbinger of the shadows' potential return.

Arjun, his hand tightening around the hilt of his sword, exchanged a worried glance with Anya. The moonlight melodies, once a source of comfort, seemed to hum with a discordant note, a warning thrumming in their very bones. This was the beginning of their story, a tale where the melody of courage would clash with the chilling symphony of fear.

Chapter 1: The Dread of Darkness

Arjun, a wisp of a boy barely scraping into his teenage years, stood trembling at the edge of the whispering woods. The late afternoon sun cast long, menacing shadows across the dusty path, and the air hung thick with the approaching chill of twilight. A low groan echoed from somewhere within the dense foliage, sending shivers down Arjun's spine. He clutched the rough wool of his tunic, his knuckles white.

Fear, a constant companion, gnawed at him. It wasn't the fear of wild animals, or the occasional rumble of thunder during monsoon season. No, Arjun harbored a far deeper, primal dread – a terror of the encroaching darkness. Every rustle of leaves, every flitting shadow, whispered chilling tales in his ears, stories passed down through generations in his village nestled at the woods' edge.

These were stories of formless creatures that lurked in the inky blackness, their touch draining the warmth and light from life itself. Stories of a malevolent entity, the Queen of Shadows, who feasted on fear and despair, forever seeking to expand her shadowy domain. Arjun had scoffed at these tales during the sunlit hours, but as dusk approached, a cold, icy hand of terror squeezed his heart.

He wasn't always this way. As a child, his days were filled with adventures in the sun-dappled meadows bordering the woods. He'd chase butterflies, climb trees like a nimble monkey, and build forts out of fallen branches, his laughter echoing through the air. But then came the night. A particularly ferocious storm raged, unleashing torrents of rain and howling wind. A stray bolt of lightning illuminated his room, momentarily revealing a grotesque, clawed shape at his window.

Though his parents assured him it was just a trick of the lightning, the image burned itself into his memory. That night, a suffocating terror gripped him, refusing to loosen its hold. From then on, the darkness became his tormentor. He would barricade himself in his room after sunset, the flickering lamplight a frail shield against the encroaching shadows.

Today, however, was different. A nagging curiosity, a yearning for the carefree days of his childhood, warred with his fear. Whispers had been swirling through the village lately, tales of a luminous light seen deep within the woods. Not a celestial glow, but a warm, inviting beacon that defied the encroaching darkness. Intrigue battled with terror in Arjun's heart. Could it be true? Could there be something beautiful hidden within the very thing he feared most?

He took a tentative step forward, then another, the dry leaves crunching ominously under his bare feet. The sun dipped lower, painting the sky in hues of fiery orange and bruised purple. The shadows grew longer, bolder, reaching out towards him like skeletal fingers. Arjun flinched, his breath catching in his throat. Every instinct screamed at him to turn back, to seek the safety of his fire-lit home.

But the image of the mysterious light, a spark of defiance against the encroaching darkness, held him back. Taking a deep, shuddering breath, Arjun closed his eyes and pictured his grandfather, a man known for his fearlessness. "There's nothing to fear in the dark, lad," his grandfather's voice would boom, "except the shadows we let control us."

With newfound resolve, Arjun opened his eyes and peered into the woods. The air hung heavy with the scent of damp earth and decaying leaves, but there was a strange stillness too, an absence of the usual nocturnal sounds. He took another step, then another, his heart pounding a frantic rhythm against his ribs. Each creak of a branch, each rustle of leaves sent a jolt of fear through him, but he pressed on.

As he ventured deeper, the oppressive darkness seemed to tighten around him. The last sliver of sunlight vanished, replaced by an inky blackness that swallowed everything whole. Panic rose in his throat, a cold sweat clinging to his skin. He stumbled forward blindly, his arms outstretched, feeling like a lost child adrift in a vast ocean.

The fear threatened to consume Arjun. He squeezed his eyes shut, willing himself to turn back, to run blindly through the woods until he stumbled upon the familiar path leading back to the village. But then, a faint sound pierced the oppressive silence. It was a melody, soft and ethereal, carried on the wind like a whisper. It wasn't a song in the traditional sense, but a series of tinkling notes, almost like wind chimes dancing in a gentle breeze.

Curiosity, a spark in the midst of fear, compelled Arjun to open his eyes. He strained his ears, focusing on the sound. It seemed to be coming from further ahead, drawing him deeper into the heart of the woods. Hesitantly, he took a step forward, his hand reaching out to brush against the rough bark of a nearby tree for support. The ground beneath his feet was uneven, a tangle of roots and fallen leaves. He stumbled a few times, but the melody remained his guiding light, pulling him onwards.

As he walked, the darkness seemed to shift slightly. It wasn't a physical shift, but a change in intensity. A faint, almost luminescent glow emanated from somewhere ahead, a soft counterpoint to the oppressive blackness. The melody grew stronger, sweeter, its notes weaving a mesmerizing spell around Arjun. He found himself walking with a newfound confidence, his fear momentarily forgotten.

He emerged into a clearing, a small, almost sacred space bathed in an otherworldly light. The source of the glow was a large tree at the center of the clearing. Its bark wasn't brown or grey, but a shimmering silver, reflecting the light with an ethereal brilliance. The leaves, instead of the usual green of the forest canopy, were a translucent white, catching the moonlight and diffusing it in a soft, milky glow.

Beneath the silver tree, nestled amongst the roots, was the source of the melody. A girl, no older than himself, sat there. Her back was to him, her fingers dancing across a stringed instrument unlike anything he'd ever seen. It was carved from a single piece of pale moonlight wood, its body shimmering with an internal luminescence, and the strings were woven from moonlight itself. As she played, the melody filled the clearing, weaving through the air like moonlight dancing on water.

Arjun stood transfixed, captivated by the sight. The light from the silver tree and the girl's otherworldly music had chased away the darkness, both literal and metaphorical. The fear that had gripped him moments earlier had evaporated, replaced by a sense of awe and wonder. He took a hesitant step forward, the soft crunch of leaves under his feet announcing his presence.

The girl turned, her movements fluid and graceful. Her hair, a cascade of midnight black, flowed down her back, catching the moonlight's glow. Her eyes, the color of deep emeralds, seemed to reflect the very essence of the forest, a captivating mix of mystery and serenity. She stopped playing the instrument, its final note echoing through the clearing before fading into silence.

"Who are you?" Arjun stammered, the words tumbling out in a rush. "What is this place?"

The girl smiled, a hint of amusement twinkling in her eyes. "This," she said, her voice soft and melodic like the music she'd played, "is a place where the darkness holds no sway. And I," she continued, extending a hand towards him, "am Reena."

Arjun hesitated for a moment, then reached out and took her hand. It was cool and smooth, and he felt a strange warmth spread through him, a spark of connection that seemed to resonate deep within him. "My name is Arjun," he said, his voice finding its strength.

Reena's smile widened. "Welcome, Arjun," she said, gesturing towards the space beside her beneath the silver tree. "Come, sit with me. Tell me what brings you to this hidden haven."

Arjun, his fear replaced by a budding curiosity, sat beside Reena. He looked up at the silver tree, its light bathing them in a soft glow. He felt safe, strangely comforted by this mysterious girl and the otherworldly magic that surrounded him. He began to tell her about his fear of the darkness, of his fight against the suffocating terror that had haunted him for so long. As he spoke, Reena listened patiently, her emerald eyes fixed on him.

When he finished, she spoke softly, her voice filled with a quiet wisdom. "Fear is a natural part of us, Arjun," she said. "But it is not meant to control us. It is a warning, a way for us to protect ourselves from danger. However," she continued, a playful glint in her eyes, "sometimes, the darkness we fear holds beauty and wonder within it. Just as the sun needs the night to exist, so too does light need darkness for its true brilliance to shine."

Reena's words resonated with Arjun, sparking a newfound perspective within him. The darkness, once a symbol of terror, now held a hint of intrigue. He looked around the clearing, his eyes adjusting to the gentle luminescence. The silver tree cast an ethereal glow, illuminating the intricate patterns on the forest floor formed by fallen leaves and moonlight. The air hummed with a soft energy, a melody of nature far different from the unsettling sounds he usually associated with the woods at night.

"But how can I overcome this fear?" Arjun asked, his voice barely a whisper. "How can I learn to see the beauty in the darkness instead of just the danger?"

Reena smiled, a gentle warmth radiating from her. "The first step," she said, "is facing your fear head-on. Not recklessly, but with courage and a willingness to learn." She gestured towards the moonlight instrument in her lap. "The music I play is a shield against the darkness," she explained, "a melody woven from moonlight and the whispers of the forest. It can help guide you, protect you from the shadows that seek to harm."

Intrigued, Arjun reached out a tentative hand towards the instrument. The moonlight wood felt cool and smooth beneath his touch, and the strings shimmered with an otherworldly light. Reena placed his hand on one of the strings, her own hand gently guiding his.

"Close your eyes, Arjun," she instructed softly. "Focus on the light, the beauty that surrounds you. Let the melody flow through you, and allow it to become a shield against your fear."

Arjun closed his eyes, his heart pounding a nervous rhythm against his ribs. He focused on the soft glow of the silver tree, the gentle rustling of leaves in the night breeze, and the ethereal melody that filled the clearing. As he did, a sense of calm washed over him, pushing back the tide of fear that had threatened to engulf him.

He felt a connection with the darkness, not of terror, but of a quiet respect. The shadows still held an element of mystery, but they no longer seemed malevolent. Instead, they felt like a canvas waiting to be explored, a world with its own secrets and wonders waiting to be discovered.

When he finally opened his eyes, a newfound determination shone within them. He looked at Reena, his voice filled with newfound confidence. "I want to learn," he declared. "I want to learn to play this music, to use it as a shield against my fear."

Reena's smile widened, her emerald eyes sparkling with delight. "That," she said, "is a journey we can take together."

A thrill of excitement shot through Arjun. The prospect of learning from Reena, of wielding the moonlight instrument as a weapon against his fear, ignited a spark of courage within him. Here, in this hidden haven bathed in ethereal light, he felt a glimmer of hope, a chance to confront his lifelong tormentor.

Reena began the lesson with a gentle touch. She explained the instrument, its connection to the forest and the moonlight. Each string, she revealed, held a different melody, a unique voice that resonated with a specific aspect of the night. There was the melody of the wind whispering through the leaves, the soft gurgle of a hidden stream, the hooting of an owl perched on a distant branch.

As Reena played each note, Arjun focused on the sound, the emotions it evoked. The wind melody sent shivers down his spine, a reminder of the unseen forces that danced through the darkness. The stream melody soothed him, its gentle rhythm a balm to his anxieties. The owl's melody, however, brought a flicker of unease. It spoke of watchful eyes in the dark, a reminder of the potential dangers that lurked beyond the clearing's protective glow.

Reena noticed his apprehension. "The darkness isn't all beauty and serenity, Arjun," she said, her voice soft but firm. "There are creatures that lurk within it, creatures that feed on fear. But the music," she continued, her hand hovering over the instrument, "can also be a weapon. It can drive back the shadows, offering a shield against those who seek to harm."

Intrigued, Arjun yearned to learn more about these creatures of the night. But Reena, sensing his growing curiosity, cautioned him. "There's a time and place for such knowledge," she said. "For now, focus on the music, on mastering the melodies that reside within each string. Let them become an extension of yourself, a voice that speaks your courage and dispels your fear."

The first tentative notes that Arjun produced were far from perfect. They were hesitant, shaky, barely a whisper against the backdrop of Reena's masterful playing. But with each attempt, a flicker of confidence grew within him. He practiced diligently, focusing on the emotions each melody evoked, channeling his fear into determination.

As the night deepened, the forest around them came alive with nocturnal sounds. The chirping of crickets, the hooting of owls, the rustling of unseen creatures in the undergrowth – all sounds that once sent shivers down Arjun's spine. But now, with the moonlight melodies resonating within him, he perceived them differently. They were no longer harbingers of fear, but a symphony of the night, a testament to the hidden life that thrived in the darkness.

The first rays of dawn began to paint the eastern sky with streaks of pink and orange. The silver tree's luminescence dimmed, replaced by the soft glow of the approaching sun. Reena put down her instrument, a satisfied smile gracing her lips.

"You've made remarkable progress, Arjun," she said, her voice filled with warmth. "The fear hasn't vanished entirely, but you've taken the first step towards conquering it. The music now flows through you, a shield against the darkness."

Arjun looked at his hands, still tingling from the touch of the moonlight instrument. A sense of accomplishment washed over him. He had faced his fear, not by running away, but by learning to understand it, to find the beauty within the darkness. He knew the journey was far from over, but for the first time in his life, he felt a glimmer of hope, a belief that he could overcome his fear and step into the unknown with courage and the music of the night as his guide.

Chapter 2: The Queen of Shadows

The rooster's crow shattered the peaceful slumber that had finally settled upon Arjun. He emerged from his room, the events of the previous night replaying vividly in his mind. The clearing bathed in moonlight, the ethereal music, Reena's gentle guidance – it all felt like a dream, a beautiful yet fantastical escape from his waking reality.

But a faint hum resonated within him, a lingering echo of the moonlight melodies. It was a comforting presence, a reminder of his newfound resolve. He approached the window, a sliver of apprehension twisting in his gut. The woods, once a source of overwhelming dread, now held a strange allure. The pre-dawn light painted the trees in soft hues of grey and blue, and the air held a crispness that invigorated his senses.

Descending for breakfast, he found the village abuzz with activity. Elders huddled together, their faces etched with worry. Villagers whispered amongst themselves, their voices laced with fear. Arjun's stomach lurched. This wasn't the usual morning bustle.

"What's wrong?" he asked his mother, her brow furrowed as she kneaded dough for flatbreads.

"It's Reena," she replied, her voice strained. "She hasn't returned from the forest since yesterday."

Arjun's heart hammered against his ribs. Reena, missing? The memory of her emerald eyes and gentle smile flooded his mind. Panic threatened to engulf him, but then he remembered the moonlight melodies, the shield against the darkness. He had to help her.

"I'm going to find her," he declared, his voice surprisingly steady.

His parents exchanged a worried glance. His father, a burly man with a thick salt-and-pepper beard, placed a calloused hand on Arjun's shoulder. "The forest is no place for a young boy, especially not alone," he said gruffly, but there was a hint of concern in his voice.

"But Reena is in trouble," Arjun insisted. "She's the only one who can help me overcome my fear. I have to find her."

The villagers, having overheard the exchange, gathered around. The elder, a wizened man with eyes that held the wisdom of countless seasons, spoke up. "The legends speak of a creature who dwells within the darkness," he said, his voice raspy with age. "A being who feeds on fear and steals the light from those who stray too close."

A collective gasp rippled through the crowd. The whispers of the Queen of Shadows, the malevolent entity who ruled the darkness, suddenly felt very real.

"But there's another story too," the elder continued, his gaze fixed on Arjun. "A story of a hidden melody, a song of courage that can pierce the shadows and weaken the Queen's hold."

Arjun felt a spark of hope ignite within him. The moonlight melodies, the weapon against fear – could they be the key to saving Reena?

"The forest is dangerous, child," the elder warned, "but you may be our only hope. If you choose to go, take this with you."

He handed Arjun a small, intricately carved wooden staff. It pulsed with a faint warmth, and an inscription in an unknown language swirled around its base.

"This staff," the elder explained, "was once wielded by a brave warrior who dared to challenge the darkness. It holds the power of the forest within it, a power that can aid you on your quest."

Arjun gripped the staff tightly, a surge of determination coursing through him. He wouldn't let his fear control him any longer. He would face the darkness, armed with the moonlight melodies and the hope of finding Reena.

Arjun stood transfixed at the edge of the clearing. Fear, a primal instinct, threatened to cripple him. The palace loomed before him, its oppressive darkness a tangible force, leeching the warmth from his skin and the hope from his heart. The staff, once a source of comfort, felt heavy in his hand, the inscription blurring in his vision.

But then, a faint memory surfaced – Reena's smile, the way her emerald eyes sparkled with determination. He couldn't give up now. He gripped the staff tighter, willing himself to face the shadows.

He took a tentative step forward, the darkness rippling like disturbed water around his feet. The discordant melody, amplified within the clearing, gnawed at his resolve. His fear threatened to drown out the moonlight melodies within him, twisting them into echoes of doubt and despair.

Suddenly, a chilling laughter echoed through the clearing. It was a sound that scraped against his bones, filled with a malice that sent shivers down his spine. A figure materialized from the inky blackness, a being shrouded in shadows, its form shifting and changing, defying definition. This was the Queen of Shadows.

"Foolish child," her voice slithered in his ear, cold and menacing. "You dare enter my domain, armed with nothing but a childish song?"

Arjun felt a wave of terror wash over him. The Queen of Shadows was everything he had feared, and more. But then, he remembered the elder's words – "a song of courage that can pierce the shadows and weaken the Queen's hold." He wouldn't let her fear tactics break him.

He closed his eyes, concentrating on the warmth of the staff, the faint hum of the moonlight melodies within him. He thought of Reena, her bravery, her faith in him. Slowly, a flicker of defiance ignited within him, pushing back the tide of fear.

With newfound resolve, Arjun raised his hand and began to play. The moonlight melodies, stronger now, filled the clearing. They were not perfect, but they carried a power that resonated through the very fabric of darkness.

The Queen of Shadows recoiled, a flicker of surprise crossing her shadowy form. The discordant melody faltered, its power waning against the onslaught of light and sound. The clearing shimmered, a battleground between light and darkness being fought through music.

As Arjun played, he noticed something strange. Whispers, faint and desperate, began to rise from within the palace walls. They were voices, trapped within the Queen's domain, their light stolen, their hope dimmed.

A surge of empathy washed over Arjun. He realized the Queen wasn't just his enemy; she was a prison warden, keeping countless souls captive in her darkness. He needed to play not just for himself, but for them – a beacon of hope in the fight against despair.

The music shifted, infused with a new purpose. It was a melody of liberation, a call to arms. The once-oppressive darkness writhed and pulsed as the moonlight notes pierced through its layers. The whispers within the palace walls grew louder, transforming into a chorus of defiance.

The Queen of Shadows shrieked, a sound of pure rage and frustration. Her form flickered wildly, struggling to contain the growing power of the music. The ground beneath Arjun's feet trembled, and cracks began to spiderweb across the clearing. The fabric of darkness itself seemed on the verge of collapse.

Suddenly, the staff in Arjun's hand flared with a blinding light. The inscription, once indecipherable, glowed brightly, revealing a forgotten language that resonated deep within him. It was a final push, a forgotten weapon against the shadows.

With a final, resounding note, Arjun unleashed the full power of the moonlight melodies, the inscription on the staff, and the collective defiance of the trapped souls. The clearing erupted in a blinding flash of light, forcing Arjun to shield his eyes. When he opened them again, the Queen of Shadows was gone, and the palace stood crumbling, its shadows dissipating into the air.

Relief washed over Arjun, a wave so powerful it nearly brought him to his knees. The clearing, once shrouded in darkness, was now bathed in a soft, golden light that seemed to emanate from the very air. The oppressive silence had been replaced by the chirping of birds and the rustling of leaves in a gentle breeze. It was as if the forest itself was celebrating its liberation.

As his vision cleared, Arjun noticed figures emerging from the crumbling remains of the palace. They were men, women, and children – villagers who had been captured by the Queen of Shadows long ago, their light stolen, their spirits broken. They blinked in the unaccustomed light, their faces etched with disbelief and a flicker of hope.

An old woman, her face lined with the stories of a life lived in darkness, approached Arjun. Tears welled up in her eyes as she spoke, her voice trembling. "Thank you, child," she said, her words echoing the sentiment of the others gathered around him. "You have brought us back from the brink."

Arjun, humbled by their gratitude, felt a warmth spread through him that had nothing to do with the returning sunlight. He had faced his fear, not just for himself, but for them. He had confronted the darkness and, armed with music and courage, emerged victorious.

Suddenly, a familiar voice broke through the gathering crowd. "Arjun!"

He turned to see Reena emerge from the trees, her eyes wide with surprise and relief. Relief washed over him, a happiness so intense it made his knees weak. He rushed towards her, engulfing her in a tight embrace.

"I was so worried," Reena whispered, pulling back to look at him. "But you did it. You faced your fear and saved everyone."

Arjun smiled, a genuine smile that reached his eyes. "I couldn't have done it without you, Reena," he said. "You gave me the courage, the music, the weapon."

Reena looked at the staff in his hand, the inscription now glowing faintly. "It seems the forest had another champion in mind," she said with a knowing smile.

News of Arjun's bravery spread throughout the village like wildfire. He was no longer the boy crippled by fear, but a hero who had faced the Queen of Shadows and emerged victorious. He had learned that true courage wasn't the absence of fear, but the will to face it, to use it as fuel for his determination.

As the days turned into weeks, the villagers who had been trapped in the shadows began to regain their strength. The forest, once a source of fear, now held a new meaning for them – a place of resilience, a testament to the power of light against darkness.

Arjun continued to visit the hidden clearing with Reena. They would sit under the silver tree, bathed in its ethereal glow, playing music together. The moonlight melodies, once a shield against fear, now held a new meaning – a promise of friendship, a celebration of courage, and a reminder that even in the darkest places, a spark of light can ignite a revolution.

Chapter 3: The Perilous Path

The victory over the Queen of Shadows brought a newfound peace to the village nestled at the edge of the woods. Arjun, once a timid boy haunted by fear, became a symbol of courage. Villagers greeted him with smiles and gratitude, their eyes filled with the hope he had rekindled. The forest, once a source of dread, now held a strange allure. It was a place of transformation, a reminder of his battle against darkness and the triumph of light.

However, the scars left by the Queen's reign were far from healed. Whispers of fear still lingered, particularly amongst the elders. The whispers spoke of residual shadows, malevolent creatures that roamed the fringes of the Queen's domain, remnants of her darkness waiting to be exploited.

One humid afternoon, as Arjun helped his father mend a broken fence, the village Elder approached them, his face etched with worry. He cleared his throat, his voice raspy with age.

"Arjun," he began, "your bravery has brought light back to our lives. But the shadows haven't vanished entirely."

Arjun straightened, a flicker of unease crossing his features. "What do you mean, Elder?" he inquired, his voice laced with a hint of apprehension.

The Elder gestured towards the woods, a dark smudge against the fading sunlight. "The Queen's creatures still roam the fringes of her fallen domain," he explained, his voice low and grave. "They are weakened, their power dampened, but they remain a threat."

A cold dread settled in Arjun's stomach. The Queen's laughter echoed in his memory, a chilling reminder of the darkness they had faced. He glanced at his father, whose hand tightened around the hammer he held. The familiar fear threatened to bubble up, but Arjun pushed it down.

"What do we need to do?" he asked, his voice firm despite the tremor that ran through him.

The Elder studied him intently. "The forest holds the answer, Arjun," he said. "Within its depths lies an ancient artifact, a source of immense power that can forever banish the Queen's lingering influence." He described a shimmering amulet, rumored to be imbued with the very essence of the sun, a beacon of light capable of repelling the remaining shadows.

"But retrieving it is no easy feat," the Elder continued. "The path to the amulet is fraught with danger, guarded by the remnants of the Queen's forces. It is a journey that requires more than just courage; it requires skills you haven't yet mastered."

Arjun exchanged a hesitant glance with his father. The thought of venturing back into the woods, into the remnants of the Queen's darkness, filled him with apprehension. But he also knew that fear wouldn't keep the village safe. The amulet, a symbol of hope, beckoned him forward.

"I'll do it," he declared, his voice resolute. "I won't let fear control me anymore. I'll face the shadows again, for myself and for the village."

The Elder's face softened with a hint of pride. "I knew you would, Arjun," he said, placing a calloused hand on his shoulder. "But remember, this isn't a journey you can take alone. You'll need guidance, training to hone your skills, and perhaps even a weapon."

Arjun's heart pounded against his ribs, a drumbeat of both apprehension and determination. The weight of the village's safety now rested on his shoulders. He looked at his father, whose face mirrored his own internal conflict – worry etched alongside a flicker of paternal pride.

"Who will guide me?" Arjun asked the Elder, his voice betraying a hint of nervousness.

The Elder stroked his beard thoughtfully, his eyes scanning the villagers who had gathered, drawn by the news of the impending quest. Finally, his gaze settled on a wiry figure standing at the back of the crowd. It was Anya, a young woman known for her adventurous spirit and her uncanny ability to navigate the woods with ease.

"Anya," the Elder called out, his voice carrying across the clearing. "Come forward, child."

Anya stepped out, her dark eyes glinting with a spark of mischief. She wore worn leather boots and a tunic that seemed more suited for exploration than village life. A hunting knife hung from her belt, its polished surface glinting in the afternoon sun.

"Anya," the Elder continued, "you possess a deep understanding of the forest's secrets. You will be Arjun's guide on this perilous journey."

Anya met Arjun's gaze with a confident smile. "Ready for an adventure, young hero?" she teased, a playful glint in her eyes.

Arjun, despite his apprehension, couldn't help but smile back. A sense of relief washed over him. Anya's easygoing nature and familiarity with the woods offered a comforting counterpoint to his own anxieties.

The Elder then turned his attention to the weapon mentioned earlier. He led them to a small hut at the edge of the village, its door creaking open to reveal a dimly lit interior.

Inside, an old blacksmith hammered away at a glowing piece of metal.

"Barnaby," the Elder addressed him, "we need your skills once more."

Barnaby, a burly man with a gruff demeanor and a heart of gold, straightened and wiped the sweat from his brow. "What needs crafting, Elder?" he rumbled.

The Elder explained the need for a weapon, something that could not only defend Arjun but also channel the power of the moonlight melodies. Barnaby listened intently, his eyes gleaming with a spark of interest.

"Something special, eh?" he muttered, stroking his beard thoughtfully. He then turned to Arjun, his gaze assessing. "Tell me, young one, how do you fight? What feels most natural in your hands?"

Arjun hesitated, unsure. He had never considered fighting before, let alone wielding a weapon. But as he thought back to his confrontation with the Queen of Shadows, a memory surfaced – the feeling of the staff pulsing with warmth in his hand, the way the music resonated through him.

"The staff," he blurted out, surprising himself. "But it's just a staff."

Anya chuckled. "Not anymore," she said, her eyes twinkling. "Barnaby here can work his magic."

Days turned into weeks as Arjun prepared for his quest. Anya took him on rigorous training sessions deep within the woods, teaching him the art of stealth, the language of the forest, and the deadliest ways to defend himself. They practiced tracking unseen creatures, navigating treacherous terrain, and recognizing the telltale signs of danger.

Barnaby, meanwhile, toiled away in his forge. The rhythmic clang of his hammer echoed through the village, a constant reminder of the task at hand. Finally, on the eve of Arjun's departure, Barnaby presented him with a weapon unlike anything he had ever seen.

It was a staff, no longer plain wood, but intricately carved with symbols that seemed to shimmer with an otherworldly light. The inscription from the previous staff was incorporated into the design, glowing faintly as if imbued with a new purpose. Nestled within the crook of the staff, replacing the worn handle, was a crescent moon crafted from a luminous crystal. It pulsed with a soft, ethereal glow, a conduit for the moonlight melodies.

Arjun held the staff, feeling a surge of power course through him. It wasn't just a weapon; it was an extension of himself, a symbol of his courage and the hope he carried for the village. With a newfound determination burning in his eyes, he looked at Anya and the gathered villagers.

"I'm ready," he declared, his voice ringing with confidence. "The time has come to banish the shadows for good."

The first rays of dawn painted the sky in hues of orange and pink as Arjun and Anya ventured into the woods. The air hung heavy with the scent of damp earth and decaying leaves, the sounds of awakening birds a welcome contrast to the oppressive silence they'd known before. Anya, her movements swift and silent, led the way, her dark eyes scanning the dense foliage for any sign of danger.

Despite his training and the comforting weight of the moonlight staff in his hand, Arjun couldn't shake off a flicker of apprehension. The shadows seemed deeper now, holding a sinister awareness of their approach. The path, barely discernible, led them through a labyrinth of trees, their gnarled branches reaching out like skeletal fingers.

Suddenly, Anya stopped, a low whistle escaping her lips. She pointed towards a trail of disturbed leaves and a faint, acrid stench that hung in the air. "Shadows," she whispered, her voice tense.

Arjun's heart hammered against his ribs. Memories of the Queen's chilling laughter and the discordant melody sent a shiver down his spine. He gripped the staff tighter, focusing on the moonlight melodies that resonated within him.

A rustling sound came from the undergrowth, followed by the low growl of a creature unseen. Anya readied her hunting knife, her lips pressed into a thin line. Two hulking figures emerged from the shadows – grotesque parodies of wolves, their eyes glowing with malevolent red light.

Adrenaline surged through Arjun. Anya lunged, her movements a blur of trained precision as she engaged one of the creatures. With a practiced flick of his wrist, Arjun raised his staff, channeling the wind melody. A powerful gust of air erupted, slamming into the second creature and sending it crashing against a tree trunk.

The battle was fierce. Anya's agility and knife skills were impressive, but the shadows were relentless, their claws tearing at her clothing and leaving bloody gashes on her skin. Arjun, fueled by the music and the need to protect Anya, wove a symphony of melodies – the wind song for swiftness, the stream song for healing Anya's wounds, and the owl song for vigilance.

He noticed a weakness. The creatures, while ferocious, seemed susceptible to the moonlight melodies. With a burst of desperate energy, Arjun channeled the full power of the staff, unleashing a crescendo of light and sound. The crystal moon pulsed with blinding intensity, the inscription glowing fiercely. The creatures shrieked in agony, their shadowy forms dissolving into wisps of darkness that dissipated into the air.

Anya leaned against a tree, catching her breath, a gash on her arm bleeding freely. But her eyes sparkled with gratitude. "Good job, Arjun," she rasped, a hint of a smile playing on her lips. "You're a natural."

Arjun felt a surge of pride, but the victory was short-lived. This was just the first encounter. They were deep within the shadows' domain, and the amulet, their ultimate goal, remained elusive.

As they continued deeper into the woods, the air grew colder, and the shadows stretched longer. The remnants of the Queen's power clung to the landscape, a constant reminder of the darkness they were fighting against. They faced treacherous ravines, navigated through fields of poisonous flowers, and evaded the watchful eyes of creatures that lurked in the undergrowth.

Days turned into a blur of challenges overcome and narrow escapes. Arjun's skills grew sharper, his connection to the forest and the moonlight melodies deepening with each hurdle surmounted. But the path seemed endless, and doubt began to creep in.

One evening, huddled around a crackling campfire, Anya noticed the strain on Arjun's face. "Exhausted, hero?" she teased gently.

Arjun sighed. "Just wondering... if we'll ever find this amulet. Is it even real?"

Anya placed a reassuring hand on his shoulder. "It's the only way to banish the remaining shadows permanently. And you," she said, her gaze filled with respect, "are the only one who can wield its power."

Her words sparked a flicker of determination within Arjun. He wouldn't let his doubts consume him. His courage, forged in the face of fear, wouldn't be extinguished. He looked into the flames, visualizing the amulet, a beacon of hope in the darkness.

"We'll find it," he declared, his voice firm. "Together."

As if in response to Arjun's resolute declaration, the forest itself seemed to shift. A break in the dense canopy revealed a faint, shimmering light emanating from a clearing ahead. Hope surged through Arjun, banishing his fatigue and igniting a renewed sense of purpose. Could this be it? Had they finally reached their destination?

With cautious optimism, Anya and Arjun crept towards the light. As they emerged from the trees, the clearing unfolded before them, a breathtaking spectacle. In the center stood a massive oak tree, its ancient branches reaching towards the sky like gnarled fingers sculpted from moonlight. Suspended from one of its lower branches, bathed in the tree's ethereal glow, was a shimmering amulet.

The amulet, crafted from a crystal that pulsed with a soft, celestial light, resembled a stylized crescent moon. Intricate symbols, similar to those etched on Arjun's staff, swirled across its surface, holding an undeniable power. It was a beacon of hope, a symbol of the light that could finally vanquish the remaining shadows.

But guarding the amulet were two towering figures unlike any they had encountered before. These were not the grotesque parodies of wolves they had faced previously. These creatures exuded an aura of pure darkness, their forms seeming to bend the light around them. Their eyes, burning with an otherworldly malice, locked onto Arjun and Anya.

Anya, her face etched with grim determination, drew her knife. "These are no ordinary shadows," she whispered, her voice tense. "They are guardians, imbued with the Queen's last vestiges of power."

Arjun gripped his staff tighter, focusing on the familiar warmth that coursed through it. Fear threatened to paralyze him, but he wouldn't give in. He had come too far to turn back now. He needed to protect Anya, to reach the amulet and banish the darkness for good.

The guardians launched themselves into a ferocious attack. Their movements were swift and deadly, their touch promising oblivion. Anya engaged one creature in a brutal dance of blade and claw, while Arjun faced the other. He raised his staff, channeling the strength of the moonlight melodies.

The battle raged within the clearing. Anya parried and slashed, her agility keeping her barely out of reach of the creature's razor-sharp claws. Arjun, fueled by desperation and the power of the staff, unleashed a symphony of sound. He blasted the creature with wind to create openings, used the stream melody to heal Anya's minor wounds, and the owl melody to pinpoint its weaknesses.

The battle was a fierce struggle, testing their skills and endurance to the limit. Just when exhaustion threatened to overcome them, Arjun noticed an opportunity. The creature, momentarily distracted by Anya, exposed its chest. With a surge of adrenaline, Arjun focused all his energy on the moonlight staff, channeling every melody he had learned.

A blinding light erupted from the crystal moon, engulfing the clearing and the guardian in its brilliance. The creature shrieked in a sound that seemed to tear at the very fabric of reality. Its shadowy form writhed and contorted before dissolving into nothingness.

Anya, panting heavily, looked at Arjun with a mixture of awe and relief. The other guardian, sensing defeat, attempted to flee but was struck down by a final blast of moonlight energy from Arjun's staff.

Silence descended upon the clearing, broken only by the ragged gasps of Arjun and Anya. They stared at the amulet, shimmering innocently within reach. With trembling hands, Arjun reached out and grasped it. The crystal pulsed warmly against his palm, a feeling of immense power coursing through him.

With the amulet in hand, they knew their journey wasn't over. They still had to return to the village, but the weight of their responsibility had lifted. They had faced the shadows and emerged victorious. As they emerged from the forest, bathed in the golden light of dawn, they knew their village was finally safe, free from the clutches of darkness forevermore. The legend of the champion who wielded the moonlight melodies and the young woman who guided him through the shadows would forever be etched in the village's history, a testament to courage, friendship, and the unwavering power of light against darkness.

Chapter 4: The Echoes of Harmony

Months had passed since Arjun and Anya's perilous quest. The amulet, pulsating with celestial light, now resided in a place of honor within the village, a constant reminder of their victory over the shadows. The air hummed with a newfound peace, and the fear that had once lurked in the shadows of the forest was replaced by a sense of security.

Arjun, no longer the timid boy, had become a symbol of courage. Children followed him around, eager to hear stories of his adventures. He spent his days exploring the forest with Anya, their bond strengthened by the shared ordeal. The knowledge of the forest and the power of the moonlight melodies felt like a second skin to him.

One afternoon, as Arjun and Anya sat by the familiar silver tree, the familiar warmth of the staff emanating a comforting glow, a tremor shook the ground. A panicked cry pierced the air, followed by the frantic clanging of the village bell.

"What's happening?" Arjun asked, his heart pounding in his chest.

Anya's brow furrowed. "This isn't right," she declared, her voice laced with concern. "The shadows were banished. What could cause such a disturbance?"

Without hesitation, they raced towards the village, the unsettling tremor continuing to rattle the ground. As they emerged from the treeline, their blood ran cold. The village square, once a bustling center of activity, was shrouded in an unnatural darkness. The once-vibrant houses stood vacant, their doors hanging open like gaping wounds.

A chilling silence hung in the air, broken only by the low, ominous growl of unseen creatures. Fear, a primal instinct he thought he had conquered, clawed its way back into Arjun's chest.

Suddenly, a figure emerged from the darkness. It was the Elder, his face etched with dread. He stumbled towards them, clutching his side, a deep gash bleeding crimson on his arm.

"Arjun," he rasped, his voice raspy with pain and fear. "The shadows... they've returned. Stronger... more malevolent."

Arjun's grip tightened around the staff, a surge of anger replacing his initial fear. He wouldn't let the darkness consume his village again.

"Where are the others?" Anya demanded, her voice sharp with urgency.

The Elder coughed, a pained grimace contorting his face. "Taken... by shadowy creatures... deeper into the forest. They said..." he wheezed, his voice fading, "they said they needed the champion..."

Before he could finish, darkness engulfed him, and he crumpled to the ground, unconscious. Panic threatened to overwhelm Arjun, but he forced himself to stay calm. He needed to act, needed to understand what was happening.

"We have to follow them," Anya declared, her eyes blazing with determination.

Arjun nodded, a cold fire burning in his eyes. He wouldn't let the shadows win again. This time, they wouldn't just banish the darkness; they would find its source and eradicate it completely.

He gripped the staff and channeled the wind melody, its familiar notes a beacon of hope in the encroaching shadows. "Let's go," he said, his voice ringing with newfound resolve. "We won't let them take our village again."

Together, Arjun and Anya plunged into the heart of the forest, the once familiar path now twisting and contorting under the weight of the renewed darkness. The music pulsed around them, a shield against the encroaching shadows, as they embarked on a new journey - one that would lead them to the heart of darkness itself, and the answer to the unsettling question: why had the shadows returned?

The forest, once a source of solace, now felt hostile. The familiar path, bathed in an unnatural darkness, twisted and turned, leading them deeper into the unknown. The tremor that had rattled the village continued, a constant reminder of the malevolent force at play.

Arjun's staff pulsed with a warm light, the inscription glowing fiercely. The moonlight melodies, his shield against the darkness, poured from him – the wind song for swiftness, the stream song for vigilance, and the owl song for heightened senses. Anya, her agility honed by countless adventures, moved with a silent grace, her eyes scanning the periphery for any sign of the creatures or their captives.

Suddenly, the air grew thick with a sickeningly sweet scent, a cloying aroma that made Arjun nauseous. As they rounded a bend in the path, the forest floor opened before them, revealing a vast cavern, its entrance pulsating with an unnatural violet light. From within came the sounds of screams and terrified whimpers – the voices of their villagers.

"The shadows... they lead here," Anya whispered, her voice tight with concern.

Arjun swallowed, a knot of dread forming in his stomach. This wasn't just a return of the shadows; it was something more, something deeper at the heart of this darkness.

"We have to help them," he declared, his resolve hardening. "But we need a plan."

Anya crouched behind a fallen log, her eyes narrowed in thought. "Remember the stories of the first Queen of Shadows?" she asked, her voice barely above a whisper.

Arjun nodded, a flicker of memory sparking in his mind. The elders spoke of a bygone era, a time before the forest held any fear, when a powerful sorcerer, consumed by darkness, became the first Queen of Shadows. The stories were shrouded in mystery, but one detail remained vivid – the sorcerer's source of power.

"A heart of darkness," Arjun breathed, the weight of the revelation settling upon him.

They needed to find the source of this darkness, the heart that powered the shadows' resurgence. But the cavern loomed before them, a gaping maw promising danger.

Anya pointed towards a narrow ledge that snaked along the cavern wall, barely visible in the dim light. "We need to get close," she said, her voice firm. "There might be a way to stop this from within."

With a cautious nod, Arjun used the wind melody to propel them onto the ledge. They clung to the rough rock face, inching their way closer to the pulsating violet light. As they got closer, grotesque figures emerged from the cavern's mouth – shadowy creatures unlike any they had encountered before. But their attention was focused elsewhere, guarding the entrance against unseen threats.

Arjun and Anya exchanged a silent understanding. They wouldn't fight their way in, not yet. They needed to get inside, to find the heart of darkness, and destroy it from its core. The moonlight melodies pulsed stronger, a shield against the growing darkness, as they navigated the treacherous ledge, their hearts pounding with a mix of fear and determination.

The pulsating violet light intensified as Arjun and Anya neared the cavern entrance. The rock face beneath their fingers grew slick with moisture, making their precarious climb even more perilous. But they pressed on, driven by the desperate cries echoing from within.

Finally, they reached a narrow crevice in the cavern wall, just above the entrance. With a shared look of determination, they squeezed through the opening, emerging into a vast cavern bathed in the sickly violet glow.

The cavern was a twisted parody of the forest they knew. Gnarled trees, devoid of life, reached towards the cavern roof, their twisted branches clawing at the air like skeletal fingers. The air hung heavy with the oppressive scent of the shadows, a cloying aroma that threatened to suffocate them.

In the center of the cavern, a colossal orb pulsed with the same violet light that had guided them. Tendrils of inky darkness flowed from it, feeding into the shadowy creatures guarding the entrance and the cage suspended above the orb. Inside the cage, their captured villagers huddled together, their faces etched with terror.

A figure, radiating an aura of pure darkness, stood before the orb, his back to Arjun and Anya. He wore a long, tattered robe, his head hooded, obscuring his features. But even from a distance, they felt the overwhelming presence of evil emanating from him.

"This is it," Anya whispered, her voice tight with tension. "The source of the darkness. The heart of the shadows."

A plan began to form in Arjun's mind. They couldn't simply attack this figure head-on – his power seemed immense. He would need to distract him, create an opening to destroy the orb and sever the root of the darkness.

He took a deep breath, focusing the moonlight melodies into a single, powerful note. It echoed through the cavern, reverberating against the walls, a defiant challenge against the oppressive darkness.

The hooded figure whirled around, his eyes burning with an unnatural purple light. He let out a guttural roar, a sound that shook the very foundations of the cavern.

"Who dares interrupt my ritual?" he boomed, his voice filled with rage and power.

Arjun stepped out from the shadows, the staff held high, the inscription glowing fiercely. "We are the ones who will stop you," he declared, his voice ringing with newfound confidence. "The darkness ends here."

The figure raised a hand, a wave of dark energy pulsing from it. The cave floor trembled violently, and Anya stumbled back, grabbing onto a rock for support. Arjun braced himself against the force, the music around him wavering but holding strong.

He knew he wouldn't be able to hold him off for long. He needed to act fast. With a surge of desperate energy, he channeled the owl melody, projecting an illusion of multiple figures charging towards the hooded figure.

Distracted by the illusion, the figure turned his attention away from the orb. This was their chance.

Anya, sensing the opportunity, took off running towards the center of the cavern. The shadows guarding the entrance, confused by the commotion, hesitated for a moment. In that split second, she reached the cage and slashed at the bars with her knife, sending sparks flying.

Arjun, channeling the full power of the staff, unleashed a final, devastating blast of moonlight energy. It struck the orb, shattering it into a million pieces. The violet light died instantly, plunging the cavern into darkness.

A scream of fury ripped through the air as the darkness within the cavern writhed. The shadows guarding the entrance shrieked and dissipated into wisps of smoke. The cage, deprived of its dark magic, crumbled to dust.

As their vision adjusted to the sudden darkness, Arjun and Anya saw the hooded figure collapse, his form dissolving into nothingness. The source of the darkness was gone, vanquished by the combined power of courage, music, and a well-timed distraction.

The villagers, freed from their captivity, emerged from the fallen cage, relief and joy washing over their faces. They rushed towards Arjun and Anya, their voices filled with gratitude and awe.

The battle was won, for now. The heart of darkness had been eradicated, but they knew the fight against shadows, in all their forms, would likely continue. But with their newfound confidence, the power of the moonlight melodies, and their unwavering bond, they were ready to face whatever came next.

The cavern echoed with the joyous reunion of villagers. Tears of relief and gratitude flowed freely as families embraced, their ordeal finally over. Arjun, Anya, and the Elder stood at the center of the gathering, exhaustion etched on their faces but a quiet pride radiating from them.

The Elder placed a calloused hand on Arjun's shoulder. "You have saved us once again, young hero," he said, his voice thick with emotion. "The forest is safe, for now."

Arjun nodded solemnly. The victory felt bittersweet. He knew the shadows, like weeds, could sprout anew if left unchecked.

"We can't let our guard down," Anya chimed in, her expression resolute. "We need to understand what caused this darkness to return in the first place. Was it a remnant of the Queen's power, or something more?"

Her words echoed a question that lingered in Arjun's mind. The hooded figure, consumed by darkness, remained a mystery. Anya's suggestion sparked a flicker of determination within him.

"We'll search the cavern," he declared, raising his staff, the inscription now glowing with a gentle, calming light. "There might be clues, remnants of the ritual, anything that can shed light on this new threat."

The villagers, their initial fear replaced by a newfound sense of purpose, volunteered to help. Together, they scoured the cavern, their movements illuminated by the soft glow of the staff. The air still held the faint, lingering stench of darkness, a grim reminder of what they had overcome.

Their search led them to a hidden chamber tucked away in a remote corner of the cavern. Inside, they discovered ancient scrolls, their edges brittle and their script faded with time. Anya, her knowledge of forgotten languages extensive, carefully examined the scrolls. Her brow furrowed in concentration.

"These are chronicles," she announced, her voice hushed with awe. "They speak of a prophecy, a time when the heart of darkness might return, fueled by a descendant of the first Queen of Shadows."

A cold dread washed over Arjun. Descendant? Did that mean the hooded figure wasn't the sole source of the darkness? Could there be more like him, waiting in the shadows, plotting their return?

The Elder, his face etched with concern, stepped forward. "This changes everything," he said, his voice raspy. "We need to prepare, not just for ourselves, but for future generations."

Arjun straightened his shoulders, a newfound sense of responsibility settling upon him. He wasn't just a village hero anymore. He was the first line of defense against a darkness that threatened to return.

"We will prepare," he declared, his voice firm. "We will study these scrolls, learn from the past, and hone our skills. The shadows may return, but we will be ready."

Looking at the faces around him – the villagers, scarred but resolute, Anya, his unwavering companion – a quiet confidence bloomed within Arjun. Together, they would face whatever darkness the future held. The moonlight melodies, a symbol of hope and courage, would continue to be their shield, a constant reminder that even in the deepest shadows, a spark of light could ignite a revolution.

As they emerged from the cavern, blinking in the sunlight that filtered through the trees, Arjun knew their journey was far from over. But with the lessons learned and the bond forged in the face of darkness, they were ready to write the next chapter in their village's history, a chapter filled with hope, resilience, and the unwavering melody of courage.

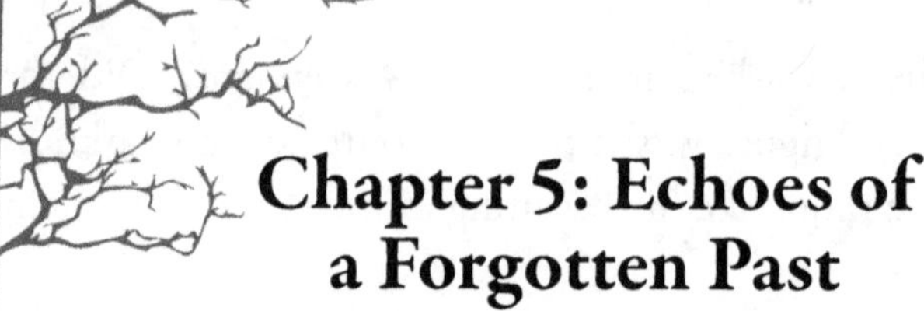

Chapter 5: Echoes of a Forgotten Past

Years flowed by like a murmuring stream, weaving a tapestry of peace and normalcy within the village nestled at the edge of the woods. The memory of the shadows lingered, a cautionary tale whispered around crackling fires on cold winter nights. But life thrummed with a newfound vibrancy, fueled by the knowledge that they had faced darkness and emerged victorious.

Arjun, no longer the timid boy, had blossomed into a man of quiet strength. The scars etched upon his arm, a memento of his battles, served as a constant reminder of the responsibility he bore. He trained diligently, honing his skills with the moonlight staff and the melodies that pulsed within him.

Anya, his ever-present companion, had become an accomplished warrior and scholar. Her agility and knowledge of the forest remained unmatched, but she also delved into the ancient scrolls recovered from the cavern, deciphering their cryptic messages and piecing together the fragmented history of the shadows.

The Elder, his hair now streaked with silver, watched over them with a mixture of pride and concern. The weight of the prophecy – the potential return of a descendant of the first Queen of Shadows – sat heavy on his heart. He knew the village needed to be prepared, not just for combat, but for the insidious whispers of darkness that could corrupt even the purest souls.

One crisp autumn morning, as the leaves swirled in a fiery dance on the forest floor, a tremor shook the ground, a faint echo of the one that had heralded the shadows' return. A hush fell over the village, a collective breath held in anticipation.

Arjun, his hand tightening around the staff, exchanged a worried glance with Anya. The tremor subsided as quickly as it began, leaving behind an unsettling silence.

"It could be nothing," Anya said, her voice betraying a hint of apprehension. "But we should investigate."

Arjun nodded, a cold knot of dread forming in his stomach. Could this be the beginning? Had the prophecy come true?

Gathering a small group of villagers, they ventured into the woods, their senses on high alert. The familiar path, once a source of comfort, now seemed to twist and turn with malicious intent. The air hung heavy with an oppressive silence, broken only by the rustle of unseen creatures and the unsettling chirping of unfamiliar birds.

After hours of cautious exploration, they stumbled upon a sight that sent a shiver down Arjun's spine. Nestled deep within a clearing stood a crumbling stone structure, its once-grand facade now marred by cracks and overgrown with creeping vines. An aura of desolation clung to it, a palpable sense of evil emanating from its very core.

"This place..." Anya whispered, her voice barely a murmur. "It's the ruins of the first Queen of Shadows' palace."

The revelation hung heavy in the air, a chilling reminder of the darkness they had faced and the one that might yet return. As they cautiously approached the ruins, the inscription on Arjun's staff glowed with an eerie intensity, a beacon of light against the encroaching shadows.

The crumbling entrance to the palace loomed before them, a gaping maw promising danger. The inscription on Arjun's staff pulsed with an urgent light, its melody a discordant warning against venturing deeper. Anya, ever the pragmatist, gripped her knife and scanned the perimeter for any signs of movement.

"This feels wrong," she murmured, her voice tight with apprehension. "But the prophecy... it could be clues about the descendant."

Arjun, his heart pounding in his chest, knew Anya was right. The shadows, if they were returning, would likely have some connection to this place, this dark legacy. He wouldn't let fear paralyze him. He had to protect his village, his home.

"We stay together," he declared, his voice firm despite the tremor in his stomach. "We have faced shadows before. We can face them again."

With a nod of agreement from Anya, they entered the palace ruins. The air inside was thick with dust and the stench of decay. Cobwebs draped the crumbling walls like ghostly tapestries, and the only light seeped in through cracks in the broken roof, casting long, skeletal shadows that danced with an unsettling life of their own.

As they ventured deeper, the air grew colder, and an oppressive silence settled around them. The passage twisted and turned, leading them down into the heart of the palace, its depths shrouded in an unnatural darkness. The inscription on Arjun's staff pulsed with a feverish intensity, the melody morphing into a frantic warning song.

Suddenly, a chilling voice echoed through the cavernous space, sending shivers down their spines. "Foolish mortals daring to tread where they do not belong."

The voice seemed to emanate from the shadows themselves, its tone filled with malice and an ancient power. Arjun and Anya instinctively drew closer, their backs pressed together.

"Who are you?" Arjun called out, his voice surprisingly steady despite the fear gnawing at his insides.

A figure emerged from the darkness, its form shrouded in swirling shadows. It was humanoid in shape, but elongated and distorted, its eyes burning with an unnatural purple light. In its hand, it clutched a staff that pulsed with the same dark energy that emanated from the ruins.

"I am a herald," the figure boomed, its voice a cacophony of whispers and screams. "A messenger of the one who will reclaim the shadows and plunge this land into eternal darkness."

Arjun's grip tightened around his own staff. This was no mere creature of shadow. This was something more - a harbinger of the coming storm.

"We won't let that happen," Anya declared, her voice unwavering despite the terror that threatened to consume her. "We will fight you. We will fight the darkness, again."

The herald threw back its head and let out a chilling laugh, the sound echoing through the ruins. "Foolish defiance! You cannot fight what is destined to be. The shadows will rise again, stronger than ever before!"

With a flick of its shadowy staff, the herald unleashed a wave of dark energy. The force slammed into Arjun and Anya, sending them flying back against the wall. The inscription on Arjun's staff sputtered, its melody faltering for a moment before regaining its strength.

Arjun knew they couldn't defeat this creature in a direct confrontation. They needed to outsmart it, to use their knowledge and the element of surprise.

He glanced at Anya, a silent exchange passing between them. They needed to create a diversion.

With a surge of determination, Arjun channeled the wind melody, summoning a powerful gust that ripped through the chamber. The force momentarily distracted the herald, who raised its staff to deflect the oncoming wind.

In that split second, Anya lunged forward, her knife flashing in the dim light. She aimed for a vulnerable spot on the herald's shadowy form, hoping to disrupt its dark energy flow.

The blade connected with a sickening thud, and the herald recoiled with a shriek. But its form wavered only for a moment before solidifying once more.

"You annoy me, mortals!" the herald roared, its voice laced with fury.

Arjun seized the opportunity. Focusing all his energy, he unleashed a powerful blast of moonlight energy from his staff. The light slammed into the herald, pushing it back and momentarily dispelling the shadows surrounding its form.

For a fleeting moment, they saw a glimpse of what lay beneath – a distorted human figure, its face contorted with rage and a darkness that seemed to consume it from within.

The revelation sent a jolt through Arjun. This wasn't just a creature of shadow; it was a person, twisted by darkness. But was there any humanity left to salvage?

The revelation hung heavy in the air, a stark contrast to the frantic pulse of the moonlight staff in Arjun's hand. The figure beneath the shroud of shadows, a distorted echo of humanity, wrestled with the darkness that threatened to consume it completely.

A flicker of doubt, a sliver of recognition, flashed in the creature's purple eyes. The herald, momentarily surprised by the combined force of Arjun and Anya's attack, staggered back.

"This power... it feels familiar..." it rasped, its voice a discordant echo of its former self.

The recognition in its voice sparked a thought within Arjun. Was this a descendant of the first Queen of Shadows, as the prophecy foretold? Or was it someone else, corrupted by the darkness that clung to these ruins?

Taking a deep breath, Arjun lowered his staff slightly, the moonlight energy diminishing to a wary hum. "Who are you?" he asked, his voice resonating with a newfound calmness. "Are you the descendant?"

The figure hesitated, its shadowy form trembling. "I... I don't remember..." it stammered, its voice a broken whisper. "The darkness... it consumes me... but there's... something else..."

Anya, ever vigilant, remained at the ready, but she too sensed a flicker of potential vulnerability in the creature. Perhaps, instead of a fight, a different approach was needed.

"Can you fight the darkness?" Anya asked, her voice gentle but firm. "Can you choose a different path?"

The figure remained silent, its form flickering between humanoid and a swirling mass of shadows. The answer seemed to lie buried deep within, a struggle between the consuming darkness and a faint spark of something brighter.

Suddenly, the ruins trembled violently. Chunks of the ceiling rained down, dust filling the air. A booming voice echoed from somewhere above, a chilling cackle that vibrated through their very bones.

"Foolish mortals! You think you can negotiate with darkness? It is inevitable!"

The herald looked upwards, a flicker of fear replacing its confusion. "Master... I have been... interrupted."

From the crumbling ceiling emerged another figure, taller and more imposing than the herald. It too exuded an aura of pure darkness, its eyes burning with an even brighter purple light.

"Failure," the figure boomed, a sneer twisting its shadowy form. "You have allowed these... insects... to live."

The herald cowered, its defiance replaced by servility. In that moment, Arjun realized this new figure wasn't just a harbinger - it was the true threat, the one manipulating the shadows, the one who truly sought to plunge the land into darkness.

But before they could react, the new figure raised its hand, unleashing a wave of dark energy that engulfed the herald. The creature screamed, its form dissolving into wisps of smoke.

"Now," the figure boomed, turning its attention to Arjun and Anya. "You will face the true power of darkness!"

Arjun felt despair grip him. They were already weakened by their encounter with the herald. How could they hope to face this new, more powerful enemy?

But then, as he glanced at Anya, a spark of defiance ignited within him. They had faced the shadows before. They had faced down a dragon of fear and doubt. They wouldn't give up now.

He held his staff high, the moonlight inscription pulsing with renewed intensity. "We will fight," he declared, his voice ringing with newfound determination. "We won't let you win."

Anya stood beside him, her eyes blazing with a warrior's spirit. Together, they faced the embodiment of darkness, ready to defend their home, their hope, and the promise of a future free from shadows. The battle lines were drawn, the melody of courage echoing within them as they prepared to face the ultimate challenge.

The cavernous chamber reverberated with the clash of darkness and moonlight. The figure, a chilling manifestation of pure shadow, launched itself at Arjun and Anya. Its movements were swift and deadly, its touch promising an oblivion colder than death itself.

Arjun, channeling the wind melody, barely managed to deflect a blow aimed at his chest. The force of the attack sent him stumbling back, his staff clattering against the dusty floor. Anya, relying on her agility, danced a precarious ballet around the creature, her blade flashing, searching for an opening.

The inscription on Arjun's staff pulsed erratically, the familiar melodies struggling against the overwhelming darkness. The wind melody, usually his first line of defense, proved ineffective against the figure's shadowy form. Despair threatened to engulf him, but he forced it down. He had to think, to find a new strategy.

Anya, momentarily distracted by the creature's relentless attacks, stumbled. The figure seized the opportunity, its shadowy hand reaching out for her throat. Time seemed to slow down as Arjun watched the scene unfold in agonizing slow motion.

Suddenly, a memory surfaced – a fragment of a forgotten scroll Anya had deciphered. It spoke of a hidden chamber within the ruins, a sanctum where the first Queen of Shadows had channeled her power. Could it hold the key to defeating the darkness once more?

With a surge of adrenaline, Arjun summoned the stream melody. A vibrant stream of moonlight energy erupted from his staff, creating a temporary barrier between Anya and the creature. He knew it wouldn't hold for long, but it bought him precious seconds.

"Anya, towards the back!" he yelled, pointing towards a hidden passage he had noticed earlier, obscured by cobwebs.

Anya understood instantly. With a desperate roll, she evaded the creature's grasp and sprinted towards the passage, disappearing into the darkness. The figure, enraged by this unexpected escape, whipped around, its shadowy form crackling with fury.

Arjun, his chest heaving, charged towards the creature, a desperate gamble. He wouldn't let it follow Anya. He would distract it, buy her more time.

The creature met his charge head-on, its shadowy form engulfing him. Arjun felt a suffocating darkness close in, draining his strength. Panic threatened to overwhelm him, but then a memory – a forgotten melody etched on the staff – flickered to life in his mind.

It wasn't a melody he had used before, its inscription faint and almost illegible. But desperation fueled his resolve. With a deep breath, he poured all his remaining energy into channeling this unknown melody.

A blinding light erupted from his staff, unlike anything he had witnessed before. It wasn't the soft, calming moonlight of the familiar melodies. This light was intense, pulsating with a primal power. It ripped through the darkness engulfing Arjun, pushing back the creature with a deafening shriek.

For a moment, there was an unnatural silence. The figure writhed in agony, its shadowy form flickering and contorting. The inscription on Arjun's staff glowed with an otherworldly intensity, the power of the unknown melody coursing through him.

Then, with a final, earth-shattering scream, the figure dissolved into nothingness. The chamber plunged back into darkness, but this time, it was the comforting darkness of an extinguished threat.

Arjun, his body trembling with exhaustion, stood amidst the silence. He had survived, but at what cost? Had he unleashed a power he couldn't control?

Suddenly, a faint call echoed from the passage. "Arjun!"

His heart pounded with relief. He hadn't been alone in this fight. Anya had made it. With renewed strength, he stumbled towards the passage, his staff a flickering beacon in the darkness.

The passage led to a hidden chamber, its walls adorned with ancient murals depicting the rise and fall of the first Queen of Shadows. Anya stood in the center, bathed in the soft glow of a single, glowing crystal.

"I found it," she said, her voice filled with awe. "The source of the Queen's power, a moonlight crystal."

Arjun approached her, his gaze drawn to the crystal. It pulsed with a gentle, familiar light, a stark contrast to the dark power he had just unleashed.

Anya held out the crystal. "This... it feels different," she said. "It feels like... hope."

Arjun nodded, a quiet understanding passing between them. They had faced the darkness and emerged victorious. But they also knew this wasn't the end. The echoes of the past would linger, a reminder that the shadows could return.

But they were ready. They had faced a new kind of darkness, and in the process, discovered a new power. With the moonlight melodies and the newfound power of the crystal, they would stand guard, protectors of ...protectors of their village and the world beyond, forever vigilant against the encroaching shadows.

The journey back to the village was long and arduous, but their hearts were lighter. They emerged from the forest, greeted by the joyous cheers of their villagers who had witnessed the tremors and feared the worst.

The news of their victory spread like wildfire. Arjun and Anya became not just heroes, but symbols of hope. The Elder, his face etched with relief, addressed the gathered villagers.

"We have faced a darkness unlike any before," he boomed, his voice filled with pride and a touch of warning. "But through courage, resilience, and the power of these two young heroes, we have prevailed."

He turned to Arjun and Anya, placing a hand on each of their shoulders. "But the fight is not over. We must study what we have learned, understand the power of the crystal, and ensure that the shadows never again engulf our land."

Arjun and Anya exchanged a determined glance. They knew the Elder was right. The crystal, with its unknown power, held both hope and a potential for unforeseen consequences. They needed to learn to wield it responsibly, to understand its connection to the moonlight melodies and the legacy of the first Queen of Shadows.

The following days were filled with activity. The villagers helped clear the entrance to the ruins, transforming it into a place of remembrance and study. Anya, with her knowledge of ancient languages, delved deeper into the deciphered scrolls, searching for clues about the crystal and its potential uses.

Arjun, drawn to the inscription on his staff that had revealed the unknown melody, sought guidance from the Elder. Together, they poured over ancient texts, uncovering fragmented references to a forgotten power – the Song of Dawn.

Legend spoke of a melody woven from the first rays of light, a song capable of not only banishing shadows but also purifying corrupted hearts. Could this be the true power of the inscription, the missing piece in their fight against darkness?

Fueled by this newfound hope, Arjun spent countless hours practicing, channeling his energy into replicating the Song of Dawn. The melody proved elusive, its notes complex and difficult to grasp. But with each passing day, he felt a connection growing, a sense that he was nearing the key to unlocking this ancient power.

As weeks turned into months, a new routine settled in the village. Training exercises became a regular occurrence, with villagers young and old honing their skills in self-defense. Anya's knowledge of the forest and ancient lore became a vital part of their curriculum.

Arjun, now regarded as a protector and a scholar, continued his pursuit of the Song of Dawn. The inscription on his staff pulsed with a renewed urgency, a beacon guiding him towards this ultimate melody.

One crisp morning, as the first rays of dawn painted the sky in hues of crimson and gold, Arjun stood atop a hill overlooking the village. He held his staff aloft, focusing all his energy. The inscription glowed with an intensity he had never witnessed before.

With a deep breath, he poured his heart and soul into the melody, channeling the very essence of the rising sun. The air crackled with anticipation as the first notes of the Song of Dawn echoed through the valley.

It was a melody unlike any he had ever heard – a symphony of light and hope, powerful and yet strangely calming. As the song filled the air, a wave of pure energy radiated from Arjun, washing over the village and the surrounding forest.

The villagers, drawn by the mesmerizing melody, emerged from their homes, their faces filled with wonder. Even the ancient trees, seemingly unmoved for centuries, swayed gently in the rhythm of the music.

Arjun continued playing, his heart swelling with a sense of accomplishment. He had finally unlocked the Song of Dawn, the melody that held the power to not just banish darkness, but to heal and restore.

As the sun climbed higher in the sky, the Song of Dawn faded, leaving behind a sense of peace and renewed hope. Arjun knew the shadows could return, but he also knew they were now prepared. They had the knowledge, the courage, and the power of the moonlight melodies and the Song of Dawn to face whatever darkness the future might hold.

The melody might have ended, but its echo resonated through the village, a constant reminder that even in the deepest shadows, a spark of light could ignite a symphony of hope.

About the Author

Mrigendra Bharti, born on June 29, 2004, in South Delhi, India, is a multifaceted individual recognized as the owner of Mrigendra Bharti Group InfoTech India Co. Pvt Ltd. Beyond his entrepreneurial endeavors, he is a distinguished music producer, director, and a budding writer.

Embarking on his professional journey at a young age, Mrigendra Bharti's visionary leadership has led to the establishment of several successful ventures, including Croma Music Series Entertainment, Sellbrochure, Fauget Innovative, and more.

What sets Mrigendra apart is his early initiation into the world of business. His foray into the unknown realms of entrepreneurship began during his 10th-grade years, where he delved into the music industry. This initial venture laid the foundation for subsequent achievements, showcasing his dedication and resilience.

Having honed his skills in music, Mrigendra Bharti not only demonstrated significant growth in his craft but also expanded his professional network. His passion extends beyond music, encompassing app and website development, as well as graphic design.

Fueled by his creative aspirations, Mrigendra established the Mrigendra Bharti Group, a company specializing in website and app development. Currently, he collaborates with a dedicated team, collectively working on ambitious projects that promise innovation and excellence.

Mrigendra's journey serves as an inspiration, particularly for today's students, highlighting the potential of youthful determination and the ability to transform innovative ideas into successful businesses. As he continues to make strides in various domains, Mrigendra Bharti remains a dynamic force, contributing vibrancy to the realms of business, music, and technology.

Read more at https://www.imwriter-mrigendra.rf.gd.